STALKED BY THE MILLIONAIRE

EMMA BRAY

Merrick

I STRIDE into the steel and glass jungle that is my office, the click of my Italian leather shoes echoing power with every step. Screens flicker to life and phones trill their siren songs as I pass, yet none of that touches the silence in my chest. Meetings stack up like a deck of cards, ready to tumble at the slightest breeze. I'm may be the man with the Midas touch when it comes to business, but when it comes to anything warm, anything resembling a heartbeat—I'm bankrupt.

I don't do distractions. I don't do close connections. People are variables in equations, predictably unpredictable, better kept at arm's length where they can be managed, controlled.

I scowl when my phone buzzes. Fucking Stephen. Always changing our meeting place at the last minute. If he wasn't a necessary associate, I'd have cut ties with him long ago. Unsurprisingly, he wants to meet at a bar. Not my scene at all, but fuck it. I just want to get this meeting over instead of playing the back and forth dance of rescheduling it a thousand times.

So, I head over to the club the dumb ass thinks is appropriate for our meeting.

Fucking idiot.

I'm still scowling when I step into the night club. I do *not* want to be here. The bass pulses through the club like a second heartbeat, and I can feel it thrumming under my skin. A kaleidoscope of lights dances across the sea of bodies, casting everyone in a flickering, multicolored glow. The air is thick with the scent of sweat and perfume, a cocktail of human desire.

I weave through the crowd, my scowl deepening when people bump into me. The patrons are a blur of hedonistic pursuit, each one chasing the night's promise of oblivion or ecstasy. Laughter rings out, sharp and sudden, while a group of women in glittering dresses takes turns sipping from a bottle of champagne as if it's mother's milk.

And then, I see *her*.

I come to a complete stop and just *stare*. I don't know what it is about her, but I can't look away.

She has a pink streak in her blonde hair that's like a beacon in the dim light, a flag of defiance in a world that tries to fit you into neat, little boxes. And it's not just the hair that catches me—it's the way she holds herself, a blend of vulnerability and steely determination that tells a story without words.

She's positively radiant amidst the chaos, her face an open book of emotions that don't belong in this place: hope, weariness, and a resilience that makes me want to step closer, to become part of her narrative.

And she's young—so young. The girl can't be more than nineteen, but her eyes tell a tale of someone much older than her years.

And something about that doesn't sit right from me.

I snap out of my daze when Stephen calls my name, hailing me over to him. I head over to the corner booth he's secured. He already has drinks waiting, but I don't touch mine.

I'm too busy watching *her* as I try to conduct business. Hell, if Stephen only knew the state of my mind right now he might could swindle me into anything. Thankfully, my reputation precedes me, and business wraps up as it should.

I watch her from the shadows of my corner booth, a

silent observer to the delicate balance she maintains between the rowdy patrons and her own guarded composure. Her laughter rings out, too loud, too bright —it's armor, I realize. The way she moves through the throng, it's graceful but deliberate. She's a swan on a pond full of snapping turtles, and every part of me wants to wade in and whisk her away.

And then she's approaching us.

My heart rate ticks up.

"Anything else I can get you?" she asks with a practiced ease, slipping the empty glasses from my table. But her eyes, they don't match the casual lilt of her voice. They're a deep blue ocean where secrets and wishes drown. There's loneliness there, a kind that echoes in the hollows of my own chest, and it strikes a chord.

"I'm good, Abby," Stephen smiles at her, and I glare at him, envious that he knows her name when I don't.

Abby.

She nods, and then those seaglass-green eyes are trained on me. They're big and beautiful and framed by thick, dark lashes. A pert little nose and lush full lips, pink cheeks flushed.

Fuck, she's like a sex doll come to life. How in the hell is every man in here not salivating at just the sight of her?

"Nothing more, thanks," I murmur, my throat tightening with unsaid words. I watch as she nods, pony-tail bobbing, the pink streak a bold slash of rebellion flicking defiantly with each step. That streak is her scream into the void, a plea for someone to see her, really see her—not just the pretty face, the body, the facade... but *Abby*. Vibrant, dreaming, struggling Abby.

Because I already know she has dreams. This girl has to know that she's made for more than *this*. They don't fucking deserve her here.

She's alone in this sea of bodies and noise, even surrounded by people. It's a loneliness I know too well—standing in a crowd, yet feeling invisible. Abby doesn't belong here, among spilled drinks and slurred come-ons. She's made for sunlit mornings and laughter that's real, for dreams that stretch beyond the smoky haze of this place.

The thought of leaving her in this world without reaching out, without knowing her story, it claws at me. But I'm the guy in the tailored suit, the one whose smile is both weapon and shield. How do I approach her without setting off alarms? Without being just another transaction in her night?

Then it hits me—a modern solution for an age-old problem. I'll find her online. It's not ideal, but it's something. A way to learn about her without scaring her off. It's innocent enough, isn't it? Just a peek into her world, nothing creepy, nothing over the line. Just...interest.

As I leave the club, I pull out my phone, fingers already tapping across the screen. Search for Abby. Which Abby is she? I scroll, heart racing, until—

There. Found her.

I'm drawn into the digital reflection of her life: pictures of her with friends, selfies that don't quite capture her spirit, vague posts about hopes and frustrations. It's a puzzle, and I'm piecing her together, pixel by pixel.

I should feel guilty, maybe, for this quiet infiltration into her existence. But the hunger to know her devours any semblance of restraint. I soak up every detail, every like, every share. I'm collecting shards of Abby, and the image forming in my mind becomes more vivid, more compelling with every click.

She doesn't know I'm doing this, and she continues to live her life unaware of my silent vigil. My infatuation blooms in the dark, fed by the glow of my phone screen. She's under my skin, and I'm lost to this obsession that whispers one dangerous, thrilling word.

More.

CHAPTER
TWO

Merrick

MY THUMB FLICKS across the screen, a relentless swiper in search of treasure. Abby's online persona is a jigsaw puzzle I'm hell-bent on solving. The blue light from my phone casts a ghostly sheen over my face as I burrow deeper into her digital life.

"Damn," I mutter under my breath, pausing at a photo of her laughing with a group of friends. She's so fucking beautiful. Everything about her captivates me. Her smile is like a hit of something forbidden, and I'm an addict craving his next fix. The pink streak in her hair stands out, a vibrant testament to her wild streak, one that I'm desperate to understand, to be a part of.

I trawl through comments, seeking clues in the banter, decoding emojis for hidden sentiments. A status update about her dog getting sick clutches at my chest. Poor thing, she must've felt so helpless. My hand itches to reach out, to offer comfort, but I restrain myself. It's enough, I tell myself, to be her unseen guardian, her secret admirer.

Meanwhile, Abby's world spins on, blissfully ignorant of my intrusion. She posts a selfie in her uniform before a night shift, her caption a simple wish for good tips. There's a tiredness in her eyes, a soft plea for respite that only I seem to notice.

"Keep fighting, beautiful," I say to the pixels on my screen, to the girl who doesn't know she's become my midnight obsession.

It's a stark contrast, her reality and mine. She's hustling for every dollar, dreams tucked into the frayed edges of her wallet, while I'm drowning in wealth and solitude. What would she say if she knew a man like me, ensnared by her spirit, was watching from afar? Would she understand this desire to be a part of her struggle, to uplift her aspirations with my own hands?

"Abby," I breathe out, the name a sacred mantra. I can't step away, not when every post tethers me closer to her. She's become my secret sanctuary, a vivid splash of color against the gray backdrop of my existence.

She goes on about her life, unaware that the

stranger from the club now follows her every online move. And as I continue my nightly ritual, scrolling, observing, *yearning*, I'm unaware that I'm teetering on the edge of something much more dangerous than mere infatuation. Abby, oh Abby, what have you done to me?

Clicking through her latest Instagram story, I can't help but chuckle at the irony. There she is, Abby, wielding a cocktail shaker like some kind of mixologist maestro, while the caption screams, "Shake it till you make it!" Her laughter is a melody in the noise of clinking glasses and chattering patrons, even though it's just a silent film playing on my phone.

The longing twists tighter inside me. The way she throws her head back, that wild pink streak flashing like a neon sign—I imagine fisting that ponytail in my hand as she takes my cock in her lips.

Fuck…

It's late, and my penthouse feels like an icebox despite the warmth of the city night seeping through the floor-to-ceiling windows. I'm perched on the edge of my designer couch, the soft leather failing to comfort the restlessness that Abby ignites in me. My thumb hovers over the heart icon, hesitating. To like or not to like? That is the question that needles at my restraint.

"Fuck it," I decide, tapping twice. A little heart blooms on the screen, a secret declaration of my fascination. It's nothing more than a drop in the ocean of adoration she receives daily, but it's a start—a crack in the dam I've built around myself.

I swipe through photos of her smile, videos of her dancing—each one a piece of the puzzle that is Abby. She's vibrant, living in technicolor, while I'm stuck in the monochrome of board meetings and silent, echoing hallways. She doesn't know it, but she's the dream I didn't dare dream—the pulse in the veins of my shadowed heart.

I trace the outline of her face on my screen with a fingertip. In my world, desire is a commodity I can afford, yet here I am, hungry for something money can't buy. Something *real*.

The clock ticks past midnight, and the silence weighs heavy. The anticipation coils, a snake ready to strike. Every night, the same ritual, the same ache. I should be content with this hidden glimpse into her life, but who am I kidding? This game of voyeuristic cat and mouse is no longer enough to satisfy the hunger she's awakened.

"Abby," I say again, rolling the name around my tongue like a fine wine. Decision claws its way up from the depths of my obsession, sharp and demanding.

I need *more*.

I want *more*.

I stand up, pacing the room, the predator within

pacing with me. My reflection in the window stares back—brooding, intense, a man on the brink of something reckless. And in that moment, I *know*.

There's a plan taking shape, a dangerous, exhilarating blueprint of pursuit. Tomorrow, I tell myself, tomorrow I'll step out from behind this screen. Tomorrow, I will find a way to bridge the gap between her world and mine.

The anticipation is a live wire, sparking with potential, with the promise of the forbidden. I go to bed with her image burning behind my eyelids, with the thrill of the chase pulsing through my veins.

The beat pounds through the walls of the club like a second heartbeat, the bass syncing with my own pulse as I push through the throng of bodies. It's a living, breathing organism this place—sweat-slicked skin and spilled cocktails anointing the dance floor. I'm a shark among the colorful fish, unnoticed yet entirely in control.

Abby's not hard to find. She's the sun in a solar system of ogling planets. The pink streak in her hair is a beacon, a defiant flare against the conformity. She moves with purpose behind the bar, oblivious to the way she captivates, the way the light plays off her curves and creates shadows I want to explore.

"Hey, handsome, lost in the crowd?" a voice purrs next to me.

"Something like that," I reply, eyes never leaving Abby. The woman laughs, a sound that wants to be seductive but comes off as trying too hard.

"Can I buy you a drink?" she tries again, leaning in, her perfume invading my space.

"No thanks," I dismiss, sharper than intended. I'm not here for small talk or flirtations that lead nowhere. I'm here for Abby, and Abby alone.

"Suit yourself," she huffs, finally taking the hint and slinking back into the mass of gyrating bodies.

I watch, entranced, as Abby deals with drunken requests and fending off hands that linger too long. There's a steel in her spine, a fire that tells me she's no damsel, but every knight has his quest, right?

And she's *mine*. My very own grail.

Time to get closer. I abandon my post at the bar and weave through the crowd, each step deliberate, calculated. There's a hunger in my veins, a craving only *she* can satisfy, and it's driving every action now.

"Another round of shots!" someone bellows as I pass, the cheer echoed by a group of partygoers who don't seem to care about tomorrow's hangover.

"Sorry, excuse me," I say absently as I bump shoulders with a couple locked in their own private world, their mouths fused together in sloppy desperation.

And then, there she is, close enough for me to smell her—a mix of sweet sweat and something floral that wraps around my senses and tugs at something primal within.

"Here's your change," Abby says to a customer, her voice a melody above the chaos, unaware of the storm she's brewing inside me. Her eyes haven't met mine yet, but when they do, I'll be ready to drown in whatever depths they hold.

"Got room for one more order?" I ask, my voice low, almost a growl, as I take the vacated spot at the bar.

She turns, and oh, those eyes. They're oceans, and I'm about to dive in headfirst.

Abby

I LOOK UP and see the guy from the other night, tall and confident, with a stride that owns the room even before his foot lands on the polished floor. There's a buzz in the air, the kind that tells you someone important just stepped in. I remember him, how could I not? But this time, it's different—no other man to share his thunder, just him, alone, radiating that silent power.

"Evening," I greet, tucking a loose strand of hair behind my ear as he settles into one of my section's booths. "What can I get you?"

"Hey." His voice is deep, smooth like aged whiskey —warm enough to send a shiver down anyone's spine.

I catch myself staring a little too long. He holds my gaze, unwavering, and there's something about the intensity in those eyes that feels like a challenge. It's as if he's not just looking at me. He's seeing right through the façade of the perky waitress.

And that unsettles the hell out of me.

"Start with a scotch, neat," he says, handing back the menu without so much as a glance at it. His attention doesn't stray, thumb brushing against the edge of the table, fingers drumming a silent rhythm. "And keep them coming."

"Sure thing," I reply, scribbling down the order even thought it's easy enough to remember. It's hard to ignore the heat that crawls up my neck under his steady gaze. Most guys come in here throwing glances like darts, hoping one will stick. But not this guy. He looks at me like he's already hit the bullseye and the game's just begun.

"Anything to eat, or are you sticking with liquid dinner?" I quip, aiming for nonchalant but feeling anything but.

"Let's see how the first course goes," he counters, a corner of his mouth inching upward in a half-smile that suggests he's not talking about the food.

"Right," I say, biting down on my lip to hide the smile threatening to break through my professional facade. "I'll be right back with your drink."

He nods, and only then does he release me from the weight of his gaze, allowing me to pivot and head for the bar. But even as I walk away, I can sense his eyes trailing after me, a silent tether pulling taut with every step.

I weave through the sea of gyrating bodies, tray balanced on my hand like a seasoned acrobat. The club's pulse pounds in my ears, a rhythm I'm all too familiar with. But it's not the bass that has my heart thumping—it's the sight of *him*, the man who seems to have an orbit of his own amidst the chaos. As I approach him, a flicker of disquiet stirs within me.

"Another whiskey, right?" I ask, even though I remember his drink from before—neat, no fuss. It's the kind of memory that comes with serving drinks to forget your own problems.

"Make it a double this time," he replies, voice smooth as the liquor he favors.

"Coming up," I say, but I linger just a moment longer than necessary. His presence is magnetic, and I can't help but recall the smug looks and empty promises of wealthy men who've sat here before him. They wear their money like armor, thinking it can buy them any heart's desire—including mine. I've learned to build walls made of ice and smiles. They're my shield against these modern-day Midases.

But this guy...he's different. He doesn't flaunt his

wealth, yet it clings to him—a subtle hint, like cologne that's expensive but not overpowering. I can't ignore the rugged edge to his attractiveness that sets every nerve ending on alert. The shadow of stubble along his jaw gives him a roguish look, the kind you'd find on a man who knows how to handle more than just business deals. His hair, dark and slightly tousled, suggests he's come straight from conquering boardrooms—or maybe hearts.

"Double whiskey. Sure thing, Mister," I remind myself out loud, tearing my gaze away from the lines that etch his strong forehead and the eyes that seem to see right through the facade most people don't even notice I'm wearing.

"Merrick," he corrects me, and my breath hitches.

I give him a tight smile and turn to go fill his order. *Get it together*, I mentally chant to myself I make his drink.

I glide back to his table, the weight of his gaze like a physical touch. It's my job to ignore it, to play it cool. "Got your whiskey," I say, placing the glass down with practiced ease. "Anything else?"

"Actually, yes," Merrick doesn't break eye contact as I straighten up. "What's good here, Abby?"

I blink, startled that he knows my name, but then again, that's not that unusual. Although we don't wear name badges, it's easy enough to learn the watiresses' names here, and he heard his friend from the other night say my name too.

"Depends on what you're in the mood for." I keep my tone light, but professional. The last thing I need is another rich guy mistaking my friendliness for something it's not.

"Surprise me." His voice is deep, a hint of amusement lacing his words as if he knows I'm trying to keep him at arm's length.

"Alright then," I retort, tapping into that flirtatious energy that makes tips bigger and nights shorter. "How about our signature cocktail? It's called 'The Maverick'. Bold, unpredictable—might be up your alley."

"Sounds like a dare." He smirks, and even though I roll my eyes, I can't help mirroring his smile just a little. "I'll take it."

"Coming right up." As I walk away, I can feel his eyes still on me, and a warmth unfurls in my chest. I squash it immediately, replacing it with the ice-cold reminder of my goals.

Because while Merrick's attention is flattering, it's not going to help get me out of this place. Every night I'm here, serving drinks, dodging hands that creep too close, I'm one step away from the life I'm desperate for —a life where control isn't just a luxury, it's my reality.

As I mix his drink, I imagine a different scene—one where I'm the boss, calling the shots, creating something of my own. The shaker feels heavy in my hand, not just with liquor and ice, but with all the dreams it represents.

"Here you go," I say, sliding 'The Maverick' across the bar to him. "Careful, it's got a kick."

"Much like its creator, I suspect," Merrick replies, lifting the glass in a silent toast before taking a sip.

"Maybe," I concede with a mysterious smile, knowing full well the most intoxicating thing I could offer him—or anyone—is a taste of the woman I'm determined to become.

I watch Merrick from the corner of my eye as he sips the cocktail, the subtle curve of his lips hinting at approval. My heart does a little dance—not that I'd ever admit it out loud. He's just a customer, albeit a distractingly handsome one with eyes that seem to strip away the noise of the crowded nightclub, leaving only the thrum of possibility between us.

"Good choice?" I ask, leaning slightly on the bar, feigning nonchalance while every cell in my body is acutely aware of him.

"Very," he says, his voice low and smooth, like the jazz humming softly through the speakers. "Though I suspect anything you create would taste like heaven."

My laugh is quick, a burst of genuine amusement that feels too intimate for the space we're in.

The moment stretches, charged with an energy

that's new and old at the same time, like a song you can't quite place but swear you've loved before. And for a second, I let myself indulge in the fantasy of it all —of being seen by someone like Merrick, someone who looks at me and sees beyond the apron and order pad.

But fantasies don't pay the bills. They don't break down the walls I've built to protect myself from silver-spooned charmers with more dollars than sense. So I straighten up, tucking away the fluttering hope that wants to take flight.

"Enjoy your drink, Merrick," I say, punctuating the air between us with a smile that doesn't reach my eyes. "Let me know if you need anything else."

He nods, and I turn away, letting the rhythm of my work pull me back to reality. The clink of glasses, the low murmur of conversations, they're my anchor in a sea of what-ifs.

As the night wears on, the promise of closing time becomes my beacon, each tick of the clock a step closer to solitude and the sanctuary of my own thoughts. Finally, the last patron stumbles out, and I'm left alone in the quiet aftermath, wiping down the bar and stacking chairs.

I want more—more than fleeting looks and hollow compliments. I want a life that's *mine*, forged from hard work and relentless drive.

One day, I'll walk out of here and never look back, stepping into a world where I call the shots, where my worth isn't determined by tips or how well I can mix a drink. One day, I'll be someone people remember, not because of how I make them feel for a night, but for what *I* achieve.

CHAPTER
FOUR

Merrick

I LEAN against the cold brick wall, a shadow among shadows, and watch her. Abby's laughter spills out into the night as she exits the pulsing nightclub, the sound a sweet melody that I'm starved for. Her hair is a wild cascade of curls, glinting under the streetlights, a stark contrast to the dark sky. She's unaware of me, but I'm hyper-aware of her—every move, every breath.

"See you tomorrow, Abby!" someone calls from the doorway.

"Night, Gina!" she responds, her voice vibrant, and it thrums through me, an electric charge.

She starts walking, and my feet move of their own

accord, keeping a careful distance. It's become a ritual, this following. It's not about control. It's the pull, the magnetic force drawing me to her presence. I can't resist it any more than I can stop breathing.

The streets are almost deserted at this hour, the only sounds are the distant hum of the city and the click of her heels on the pavement. I slip in and out of the dim pools of light cast by the street lamps, my steps silent, my heart pounding an erratic rhythm. It's like a dance —the way I move with her, always just out of sight.

I've learned the route by heart, know every shortcut and alley she might take. Yet she never deviates, a creature of habit, just like me.

She grips her keys tightly in her hand and glances about her every so often, making sure to stay aware of her surroundings. She's cautious, smart. It's one of the million little things I find endearing about her.

As she slips into her building, I feel the loss immediately, the absence of her like a physical ache. The craving returns, gnawing at my insides, the obsessive need to be close to her, to make sure she's safe.

I stand vigil outside her apartment all night, dreaming of her, *obsessing* over all the things I'd like to do to her.

And it's not all sexual, though I'd be lying if I didn't say much of it is. Sure, I dream of seeing her puffy, pink lips wrapped around my cock, but I also dream of holding her in my arms and just watching her while she sleeps, of brushing a stray lock of hair off her forehead.

Little things I've never daydreamed of before.

And when she finally leaves in the morning, I make my move.

The lock clicks, a soft surrender to my practiced hands. I step inside Abby's apartment, a place that breathes her essence even in her absence. The silence wraps around me like a familiar cloak as I move with purpose, the weight of my backpack heavy with its illicit cargo.

My fingers are nimble as I extract the tiny cameras from their protective casing. They're sleek, unassuming —perfect for my little project. A buzz of adrenaline spikes through me, a cocktail of excitement and guilt, as I plant the first camera behind a cluster of books on the shelf. High enough to survey the room, angled just right.

I glance at her worn sofa and imagine her curled up on it, lost in one of her romance novels. Does she ever fantasize about a man like me watching over her? Protecting her?

I install the next camera in the hallway, another in the kitchen. I know her routine like the back of my hand—the early morning coffee, the late-night snacks. Every part of this small, shabby apartment gets a pair of electronic eyes. It feels wrong and right all at once—wrong to invade her privacy, but right to ensure she's always in my line of sight.

I stand in the center of her living room, done with my task. My gaze wanders over the patched-up furniture, the secondhand TV, the pile of bills that threatens to topple over the edge of the counter. This isn't the life she deserves. Hell, it feels like a crime that someone as vibrant as Abby has to come back to this every night.

A surge of frustration tightens my jaw. She hustles in that club, pouring drinks for leering men who will never appreciate her true worth, while I... I'm useless, hiding in the shadows. But not for much longer. I clench my fists, a silent vow etching itself into my bones—I'll lift her out of this, give her the stability and comfort she's been denied.

I slip out as quietly as I came, locking the door behind me with a soft click. The night air hits my face, sobering, as I walk away from her building. Abby's unaware of the guardian angel lining her pockets with miracles, but soon, she'll feel the warmth of my secret embrace, lifting the weight of the world off her delicate shoulders.

———

I crack my knuckles and lean into the glow of my laptop screen.

"Okay, Merrick, think," I mutter to myself, tapping a rhythm against the keyboard. "How do we play fairy godmother without the damn glittery wand?"

A quick search pulls up a dozen ways to be someone's financial ninja. Anonymous donations, charity funds, scholarships... My eyes skim the list until they snag on something that resonates with a deep, throbbing hum inside me. Debt relief. That's where I'll start.

"Let's erase those numbers, sweetheart," I whisper, as if she's right here with me, her legs draped over mine, lips curled in that secret smile she saves for the end of a hard shift.

Clicking through her accounts feels like I'm peeling back layers of her life. Each bill is a weight she carries, a shadow under those bright, too-knowing eyes. Medical bills from before I knew her, credit card debt piling up like dirty snow. It's a mountain of 'due by' dates that no one should have to climb alone.

"Time to avalanche this shit away," I say, adrenaline pumping hot through my veins.

The bank asks for confirmation, and my finger hovers over the mouse. There's a thrill in this, a rush of power knowing I can wipe her slate clean with a single click. But it's more than that—it's a promise, an unspoken pact between me and the universe to keep her safe, to lift her up when she doesn't even know she's falling.

Click.

And just like that, her debts disappear into the digital ether, sucked away by my silent intervention. She won't wake up to fanfare or a golden ticket. Instead, she'll find zero balances, quiet notifications that don't quite add up but spell relief in every language.

I imagine her confusion turning to disbelief, then joy. And I'll be there, watching, *burning* with the need to tell her it was me, that I'd burn the world down just to see her smile.

But not yet. Not now.

I rub a hand across the stubble shadowing my jaw.

The night stretches on, endless and still, but for the first time in weeks, I let myself lean back in my chair with a grin splitting my face.

But then I frown. I may have wiped her past slate clean, but what about her future?

The neon glow of the computer screen flickers across my face, casting long shadows against the dark walls of my study. I tap a rhythm on the desk with my fingers, a countdown to the moment Abby's life takes another turn for the better. At least, that's the plan.

"Six months," I murmur, doing the math in my head. Six months without the fear of coming home to an eviction notice plastered on her door. It's not a lifetime, but it's a damn good start.

I pull up the contact information for Abby's landlord, one I've meticulously gathered without raising any suspicions. A few clicks, a secure phone line, and I'm through, my voice a disguised baritone that's as untraceable as it is authoritative.

"Good evening. I'd like to discuss a tenant of yours —Abby Sinclair," I say, keeping my tone casual, detached.

"Is there a problem?" The landlord's wary voice crackles through the speaker.

"Quite the opposite," I assure him. "I represent an interested party who wishes to ensure Ms. Sinclair's continued tenancy. We'd like to pay her rent for the next six months. In full. Anonymously."

There's a pause, a silence that stretches just a touch too long. But then comes the capitulation, the sound of greed greasing the wheels of cooperation. "I see no issue with that. As long as the funds are transferred."

"Consider it done," I reply, ending the call with a smirk. My pulse thrums with anticipation. Abby won't have to stress for a roof over her head—not anymore.

"Step two," I breathe out, cracking my knuckles before they fly over the keys once more. An anonymous email address, a few strokes of genius, and I'm one click away from dangling a lifeline in front of her—

a job opening at my firm. She's smart, she's capable, and damn it, she deserves more than the hand she's been dealt.

I craft the email and send it, my heart racing faster at the click of the button.

The promise of seeing her every day, of being near enough to catch the scent of her hair or the sparkle in her eyes—it's a heady thought. And as dangerous as it is desirable.

But I shove those thoughts aside. Because this isn't about me. It's about Abby. About giving her the world, even if I have to do it from the shadows.

CHAPTER FIVE

Abby

I'M STARING at my battered laptop, the glow of the screen casting long shadows across my tiny studio. Skepticism crawls through me as I reread the email that popped up in my inbox, an eyebrow arching in disbelief.

The cursor blinks back at me, a silent challenge. Could this be legit? Or is it just another scam preying on the desperate?

I glance over at the mounting pile of bills on my table and bit my lip. Because I *am* desperate, and desperation makes you do funny things.

Like hope.

"Ah, what the hell," I say with a click of my tongue, fingers flying over the keys. Curiosity's got me by the throat, and I'm not one to shy away from a dare—even if it's from a faceless stranger. I fill out the application with a mix of trepidation and a wild flicker of excitement.

Here goes nothing.

———

The day of the interview arrives like a freight train—loud, fast, and impossible to ignore. I step into the sleek lobby of the firm, my heart pounding a staccato rhythm. This is all so surreal. I don't think I really expected to hear back after responding to the email.

The receptionist calls my name, and I nod, smoothing down my best (and only) pantsuit.

I follow her down a corridor lined with glass offices, everything shining and intimidating as all get-out. And then we stop at a door more imposing than the rest, and she gestures for me to go in.

"Mr. Merrick Mason will see you now."

Merrick. The name jolts through me like a live wire. *No. It can't be.*

But as I step inside, there he is—Merrick Mason, every inch the brooding, intense enigma I remember from fleeting encounters that left my skin tingling. His presence fills the room, a magnetic force that draws my gaze and holds it captive.

"Abby," he says, a ghost of a smile playing on those ridiculously kissable lips. "Please, have a seat."

I sit, but my mind's racing. Gratitude wars with suspicion, and it's a bloody battle.

"Surprised?" Merrick's voice is low, a smooth caress that's somehow both comforting and unnerving.

"Understatement," I shoot back, clinging to my usual sass like a life raft. "What's the game, Merrick?"

"No game." His gaze never wavers, dark and inscrutable. "I saw potential in you, Abby. That's all."

"Potential," I echo, the word feeling foreign on my tongue. It's hard to trust, harder still when it's Merrick offering the olive branch. But damn if I don't want to believe him.

"Take a chance on me," he says, and it's not a question. It's a plea wrapped in velvet steel.

So here I am, torn between the heat in his eyes and the cold feet dancing a jig in my stomach. I've always been a gambler at heart, though. And something tells me betting on Merrick Mason might just be the wildest ride yet.

———

Merrick

. . .

"Congratulations, Abby. You're hired." My words hang between us, crisp as a freshly printed contract.

She blinks, her eyes wide with a cocktail of shock and elation I've come to crave. The corners of her mouth twitch, fighting a battle against the gravity of disbelief before surrendering to a smile that hits me in the gut. Hard.

"Really?" Her voice is a mix of hope and wariness, a siren's call wrapped up in caution tape.

"Really," I affirm, letting the word roll off my tongue like a promise.

I lean back in my leather chair, the material creaking under the shift of my weight, mirroring the tension that coils within me. As she stands there, clutching her purse like a lifeline, I can't help but revel in the fact that she's mine now. Not in the way I want—no, not yet—but as close as I can get while still playing by society's rules.

"Welcome to Mason Enterprises, Abby. I expect you bright and early on Monday," I say, unable to keep the edge of command from seeping into my tone. It's a tone that says more than welcome aboard—it whispers of late nights and shared secrets, of a future teetering on the brink of possibilities.

"Thank you, Mr. Mason. I... I won't let you down,"

she stammers, sincerity bleeding through her usually fierce exterior. She's vulnerable, open, and it makes me want to shield her from every shadow that's ever darkened her world.

"Merrick," I correct her. "Call me Merrick."

She stares at me for a moment as if she's trying to figure me out before she finaly nods.

As she turns to leave, her scent—a heady blend of jasmine and something uniquely Abby—lingers, teasing my senses. I watch her go, each step she takes away from my office tightens the invisible string that's tethered me to her since the moment I saw her.

I'm entranced by the sway of her hips, the determined set of her shoulders. She's oblivious to the weight of my stare, to the intensity of my focus. But that's how it needs to be—for now.

It's a fraught line I walk, this razor's edge between watching over her and stalking her. But as her new boss, I'm afforded a front-row seat to the unraveling of Abby's layers, each one peeled back revealing more of the enigma that fuels my desire.

The office door clicks shut, sealing her departure, but not the yearning that pulses through me. It's a craving that goes beyond the flesh—it's a hunger for her trust, her laughter, her light.

I lock my office door, the click echoing too loud in the silence. The fluorescent lights buzz overhead, a stark contrast to the warmth Abby's laughter brought into this sterile space just minutes ago. My fingers skim over the desk where she sat, the wood still holding the ghost of her heat.

Get it together, man. I internally chide myself, but it's no use. She's under my skin, a delicious itch I can't—and don't want to—scratch away. My thoughts are a jumble of longing and schemes, each more daring than the last, all for one purpose: to wrap Abby in a cocoon of happiness.

I flick off the lights and stride toward the tinted glass wall overlooking the city. Skyscrapers sparkle like fallen stars, each light a beacon of dreams just out of reach. But not for Abby. Not if I have anything to say about it.

"Damn it, you're going to have it all," I whisper fiercely into the darkness, my reflection staring back at me with an intensity that matches the storm brewing inside.

The walk home is a blur, my mind racing faster than my feet. I can't shake the image of Abby in that interview chair, poised on the edge of a new life, her eyes alight with cautious hope. She's a fighter, my fierce little phoenix rising from the ashes of hardship.

Back in my apartment, the city's pulse fades into the background as I pour myself a drink. The amber liquid swirls in the glass, mimicking the color of her eyes—

the eyes that don't quite trust me yet. It's a challenge I accept with relish.

I sink into the leather couch, the weight of my vow settling around me. It's heavy, binding, a promise that threads through my very soul. I will do whatever it takes for Abby.

The city sleeps but I'm wide awake, plotting and planning. I'll build her a fortress of joy brick by brick if I have to, fight off any shadows that dare creep close. And when she smiles, free from worry, free from doubt, it'll be brighter than any skyline.

And for the first time in a long while, I let myself believe in a future that might just be bright enough for both of us.

CHAPTER
SIX

Abby

THE MOMENT I step out of the elevator, my heart's already doing a salsa in my chest. First day jitters, mixed with the kind of thrill you get right before a rollercoaster drop. I pause outside his office door, smoothing down my pencil skirt and taking a deep breath. The brass nameplate glints at me: Merrick Mason, CEO.

Oh boy.

"Get it together, Abby," I mutter under my breath, forcing my hand to turn the doorknob before I can bolt for the hills.

I stride in, all feigned confidence and rehearsed

smiles, but the sight of him—Merrick Mason—leaning back against his desk like he owns gravity. And damn, does he wear it well. He looks up from his papers, and that smile of his hits me like a shot of tequila—smooth with a potent afterburn.

"Abby, right on time." His voice is dark chocolate, rich and sinful. "Welcome to the team."

"Thank you, Merrick," I let his name roll off my tongue, playing it cool even though my insides are a fizzy soda pop.

That smile again, and I swear the temperature in here spikes a few degrees.

The air sizzles between us, laced with something more than just employee-boss decorum. I catch the way his eyes—a stormy blue that could drown me if I'm not careful—linger a little too long.

"Hope you're ready," he says, and it's not lost on me, the double entendre hanging in the air like an invitation.

"Always," I shoot back, the flirtatious edge to my voice surprising even me.

He chuckles, a low sound that rumbles through the room, and pushes away from the desk. As he steps closer, the space between us crackles, charged with something untamed and electric.

"Good to know," he purrs, his gaze bold and

unapologetic. "I have a feeling we're going to get along just fine, Abby."

Oh, I think to myself, heat creeping up my neck, we'll get along alright—dangerously so.

The room is intimate, almost cozy, with our desks sitting less than an arm's length apart. The air feels charged, thick with unspoken promises and the ghost of our flirtatious exchange.

I settle into my chair, acutely aware of Merrick's presence just a few feet away. His focus is on his screen, but I can feel the weight of his gaze, heavy and warm, like a blanket I'm not sure I want to shrug off.

"Merrick," I call, "can you come take a look at this?" I can't figure out this one task he's given me and want to make sure I'm doing it right

"Sure." He rises, closing the distance between us in three short steps. His presence dwarfs me as he leans over my shoulders. I catch a whiff of his cologne, something woodsy and subtly spicy. It's intoxicating.

He points at the file on my screen, but it's just pretense. We both know it.

"Here?" His finger brushes the document lightly, and then, accidentally-on-purpose, grazes the back of my hand. A jolt shoots up my arm.

"Yes," I confirm, my throat dry.

"Exactly there," he confirms. His voice is low, husky.

Our eyes meet, and there's no mistaking the flicker of heat in his. He's playing with fire, and so am I.

"I think I got it," I swallow thickly.

He straightens up but doesn't move away, the tension coiling between us, delicious and daunting.

He goes back to his desk, and I stay at mine, trying to focus on my tasks, but I feel his gaze heavy on me.

The day unfolds like a game of chess, each move calculated, each word laced with double meanings. Merrick leans across me to grab a pen, his arm brushing mine, lingering just a heartbeat too long. Our fingers tangle briefly as we exchange papers, and every touch sends my heart racing like a drum solo.

"Accidental" brushes become our language, a dialogue written in the silent spaces and the static that crackles when we're too close.

"Need help with that stack?" Merrick offers, gesturing to the pile of folders on my desk.

"It's your call, boss," I grin, watching as he scoops up half the load. His hand brushes mine again, and this time, neither of us pulls away immediately. There's an audacity in his touch, a silent challenge.

"Always ready to rescue a damsel in distress," he quips, his tone light, but his eyes are dark, stormy seas threatening to pull me under.

"Who says I'm in distress?" I tease back, leaning in

just enough to make him aware of the curve of my hip, the softness of my blouse. "Maybe I like a bit of chaos."

"Chaos can be…exhilarating," he murmurs, stepping closer, the word hanging heavy and ripe with suggestion.

The banter continues, each remark more daring than the last, steeped in innuendo until the air is thick with it. Laughter comes easy, but it's a cover for the crackling energy that builds with every passing second. It's a dance, a push and pull that's all rhythm and no rules.

"Careful, Merrick," I warn playfully, my pulse hammering in my throat. "You wouldn't want to start something you can't finish."

"On the contrary, Abby," he counters, his smile wicked. "Finishing what I start is exactly what I intend to do."

And God, the promise in those words sends a thrill racing through me. Every cell in my body is awake, alive, and screaming for one thing: *more*.

CHAPTER
SEVEN

Abby

THE CLOCK TICKS PAST THREE, the sound a metronome to my racing heart. It's as if time syncs with the pulse of desire that thrums between Merrick and me. With each hour that passes, the office feels smaller, our shared space an intimate cocoon where glances are currency and words are laden with double meanings.

I shuffle papers on my desk, pretending to be engrossed in work, but my gaze betrays me, flicking up to steal a look at him. Merrick is leaning back in his chair, eyes on his computer screen, seemingly focused. Yet, I catch the way his glance darts toward me, quick and sharp like a spark. He's watching me too, this clandestine game heightening with every stolen glimpse.

"Abby, could you come here for a moment?" His voice slices through the electric hum of tension.

"Sure," I reply, voice steady despite the somersaults inside me.

As I approach, he points to a document on his screen, but the pretext is thin, translucent. Our fingers brush when he hands me a pen, a jolt shooting up my arm. His eyes lock onto mine, dark and smoldering, and I drown in them, willingly.

"Is everything all right?" I manage to ask.

"Perfectly," he says, but there's an edge to his voice, a low growl that suggests otherwise.

Time stutters. The air shimmers with unspoken promises, and just like that, Merrick stands, closing the gap between us with a predator's grace. My breath hitches, caught in the sudden storm of his presence.

"Abby," he murmurs, and it's not a question but an invocation.

"Ye—"

His mouth crashes onto mine before I can even breathe out his name, cutting off any pretense of resistance. His kiss is fierce, claiming, an unleashing of all the pent-up hunger we've been dancing around since morning. The taste of him is intoxicating, a mix of coffee and something darker, more primal.

My hands find their way to his hair, tugging him closer, desperate to feel more of him. His arms wrap around my waist, pulling me into the solid heat of his body. Every touch is fire, every graze of his lips a brand. We're two flames, merging into an inferno that threatens to consume us both.

"God, Abby," he groans against my mouth, his voice rough with need.

The world narrows down to the space where our bodies meet, hot and unrestrained. With each passing second, the heat between us builds, a crescendo that promises to shatter all semblance of control.

And I don't care. I don't care because nothing has ever felt so right, so inevitable, as this moment with Merrick.

He threads his fingers through my hair, tugging me closer—if that's even possible. My hesitation evaporates like mist under the blaze of his touch. There's no space for doubt when every cell in my body screams his name.

"Abby," he growls, our lips parting only to steal quick breaths before crashing together again. "You're killing me."

"Good," I pant, my voice laced with a challenge. His hands map the contours of my body with a possessiveness that sends shivers down my spine. With each brush of his fingertips, he claims territory, leaving a trail of fire in their wake.

Without missing a beat, he hoists me up, and papers flutter to the floor as we make room amidst the scattered office supplies.

The cool wood of the desk presses against my back, a stark contrast to the heat radiating from Merrick's body as he leans over me. The edge digs into my skin, but it's nothing compared to the urgency of his kisses, deep and demanding, as if he's trying to memorize the taste of me.

"Fuck, Abby." He breathes the words over my neck, his teeth grazing the sensitive skin there, sending a jolt straight between my legs.

"More," I urge, arching into him, desperate for contact. Our clothes are a frustrating barrier, but not for long. He makes short work of the buttons on my blouse, his gaze darkening at the sight of lace beneath.

"Jesus, you're beautiful," he murmurs, and it sounds like a confession—one that has me spiraling into bliss.

"Show me," I whisper, feeling bold and reckless under his intense scrutiny. I'm drunk on Merrick, on the sheer force of our connection that turns the mundane office into an erotic canvas.

We improvise, our movements unrehearsed but perfectly in sync. A stapler clatters to the floor, forgotten, as he lifts me onto the photocopier, the glass cold and strangely thrilling against my heated skin. The whir and click of the machine adds a bizarre sound-track to our escapade, a reminder of where we are—a place of business turned den of indulgence.

"Look at us," he commands, flicking the machine on. And we do. The greenish light of the copier casts a surreal glow over our entwined bodies, capturing this moment of pure hedonism in black and white.

"God, Merrick," I moan, as his mouth descends once more, his tongue tracing the line of my collar-bone. Each stroke is a word unsaid, an emotion unfurled—raw, unedited passion that knows no bounds.

"Tell me what you want," he demands, his voice thick with lust.

"Everything," I reply without hesitation. "I want everything with you."

And that's all it takes for Merrick to completely snap. He thrusts inside me with a roar and fucks me furiously.

"Fuck, Abby." He breathes these words across my neck, teeth scraping against hypersensitive skin there, electrifying a shockwave that courses straight to the very core of me.

"Merrick!" I gasp out his name as he hits something deep inside me that makes my eyes roll back in my head.

"Jesus, you're exquisite," he pants, a confession that spirals me into euphoria.

And then something explodes deep inside me, and I'm shattering, clinging to him as I cry out.

"Yes," he croons. "That's a good girl. Yes, baby, let me feel that pussy come all over my cock. Oh fuck."

He plunges into me harder and faster and then he groans as he releases his seed into me in a spurt of hot warmth. He holds himself deep inside me as he continues to pulse until I feel his cum trickling down my ass.

Panting, my back pressed against the cool surface of the desk, I watch Merrick straighten his tie. His chest heaves slightly, but unlike me, he doesn't seem to be grappling with an onslaught of emotions.

"Wow," I breathe out, trying to steady myself, feeling the sticky evidence of our liaison cooling on my skin.

"More than 'wow,' Abby," Merrick says, eyes gleaming as he steps closer, his hand reaching out to brush a lock of hair from my face. "That was fucking incredible."

I should be basking in the afterglow, but instead, a tide of shame washes over me. My gaze drops to the floor, where a few scattered papers serve as a reminder that this is not a bedroom—it's an office, and I've just crossed a line I can't uncross.

"Hey." Merrick tilts my chin up, forcing me to meet his eyes. "Don't start second-guessing this."

I want to argue, to tell him we've made a mistake, but his thumb traces my bottom lip, and for a moment, I'm lost again.

"I... We can't just—" I stutter, my voice a mere whisper, betraying the whirlwind of emotions inside me.

Merrick's laugh is low and carefree, filled with the kind of self-assurance that only someone like him possesses. "To hell with everyone," he declares, his arms encircling my waist, pulling me flush against him.

"But you're my boss," I manage, the words feeling hollow even as they pass my lips. "

"So?" he says, his confidence infectious. "That's right. I'm the boss, Abby. I call the shots here. And right now, all I care about is how good you feel in my arms."

For a moment, I let myself get swept up in his conviction, in the sheer force of his presence. He's right. The world outside these walls doesn't exist—not when he looks at me like I'm the only thing that matters.

He pulls me against him, and I relax in his hold.

"That's a good girl," he praises me, his mouth curving into a smile. "Because I'm going to take care of you now. Forever."

And somehow, despite the risk, despite the voice in the back of my head screaming caution, I find myself smiling back.

Because I feel happier and safer in Merrick's arms than I've ever felt in my entire life.

CHAPTER
EIGHT

Abby

"PAID IN FULL? For six months? Are you sure?" I question my landlord.

"Absolutely sure, Abby. Now, you're good for six months." He sounds annoyed with me and is speaking to me as if I have comprehension issues—which I feel like I do right now becuase who the hell would pay up my rent like this? There has to be some mistake, but one more look into my landlord's annoyed face, and I decide I'm not going to look a gift horse in the mouth. Even if there was a mistake, it's obviously been in my favor.

So, fuck it. I head upstairs to my apartment.

The click of my apartment door shutting behind me feels like the final note in a symphony of relief. I'm home, finally, after a day that's been too long and too much.

I kick off my shoes, the freedom for my toes almost orgasmic, and toss my bag onto the nearest chair. It lands with a satisfying thud, like it's as tired as I am. My little sanctuary welcomes me in silence, dimly lit and familiar. But as I pad through the living room, something catches my eye—a soft, rhythmic blinking from the bookshelf.

"What's this?" I murmur. The blinking light is coy, a technological wink that feels entirely out of place against the backdrop of dog-eared novels and potted succulents. I approach, curious.

And there it is, nestled between 'Pride and Preju-dice' and a snow globe—a camera. A tiny, black eye watching me. My heart jackhammers against my ribcage, a drumroll of shock that quickly gives way to a hot flush of anger. Someone has been spying on me.

"Son of a bitch," I hiss, plucking the camera from its nook. The anger is a living thing inside of me now, a coiled serpent ready to strike. Who would do this? Who *could* do this?

And then I go completely still. My rent paid in full for six months. I rush over to my beat-up old laptop and log into my deliquent accounts. My eyes widen when I see them all paid in full.

Someone has paid off all my accounts. Someone has cameras in my apartment.

There's only one someone I can think of with the means to do this, and that someone swims into my mind's eye.

Merrick.

Merrick with his smoldering gaze that seems to strip me bare, his intensity that both thrills and terrifies. It makes a twisted kind of sense; he's got the means, the motive, the opportunity.

"Damn you, Merrick," I breathe, my fingers tightening around the camera until my knuckles blanch. He's crossed a line, a line that can't be uncrossed. How did we go from flirty banter and lingering looks to this invasion, this violation?

The initial shock begins to wear off, leaving a cold determination in its wake. I need answers, and I need them now. But first, I'm going to rip this place apart until I know all his dirty little secrets. If Merrick thinks he can play Big Brother with me, he's got another think coming. And when I confront him, oh, he better be ready for the storm that's about to hit.

My chest heaves, every breath like a stab of ice as I whirl around the room. The thought that there could be more—more eyes, more secrets—sends my pulse into overdrive. My gaze darts to every corner, every shadow. There it is—a faint, ominous blink near the window. Another camera, another chunk of trust ripped away.

"Son of a bitch," I mutter, snatching the second device with trembling hands. My sense of security shatters like glass under a boot heel.

The fury boils over, scalding my insides. Without hesitation, my fingers claw for my phone, the screen lighting up with Merrick's name. It feels toxic now, like I'm dialing up the devil himself.

"Abby, I—" Merrick's voice doesn't even get to finish before I cut through it, sharp as a knife. He doesn't even try to deny anything. In fact, he answered the phone like he already knew what was coming, and of course he did. He probably watched as I discovered his deceit.

"Explain yourself, Merrick!" I shout into the phone, my voice quaking with rage. "Explain why you've been spying on me! In my own home!" There's no holding back the torrent of emotions, all the betrayal and disgust pouring out of me in a venomous wave.

"Abby, please just listen to—"

"No, you listen!" I interrupt, seething. "I don't know what twisted game you're playing, but I want no part in it. I trusted you! And you..." I choke on the words, each one laced with poison. "...you've been watching me like some...some pervy peeping Tom!"

"Abby, if you'll let me explain—" His voice tries to weave regret into the words, but I'm not buying any of it.

"Save it, Merrick." The air rushes from my lungs in a hiss. "You can't undo this."

I stand there, blood boiling in my veins as Merrick's confession spills from the phone's speaker. His voice is a tangled mess of regret and desperation, but it's like trying to stitch up a wound with barbed wire.

"Abby, I only wanted to keep you safe," he pleads, his words dripping with a desperation that tugs at my heart, but I quickly harden it again. "I couldn't bear the thought of something happening to you when I'm not around."

"Safe?" I spit the word out like it tastes foul. "You think violating my privacy makes me feel safe? I'll have you know I was doing just fine on my own, Merrick. I didn't need you to pay off all my debts. I didn't ask you for any of that. And just what was that, anyway? Some sort of payment for the office fuck?" My hand clenches around the phone, knuckles white.

There's a pause before Merrick explodes. "How could you think that? Abby, I would never, ever treat you that way! You are everything to me. Everything! I only ever wanted to protect you—"

"Protect me?" I cut him off, voice slicing through the air sharp as a knife.

"Abby, just—"

"Goodbye, Merrick." The words are a stone sinking in the pit of my stomach as I end the call. I throw the phone onto the couch, watching it bounce off the cushions. My heart is a wild thing in my chest, thrashing against its cage. A tiny victory courses through me, but it's short-lived against the tide of betrayal.

The room feels suddenly too small, walls closing in on me. I take a deep breath, finding a sliver of composure amid the chaos raging inside. My laptop sits on the desk, innocently unaware of the bombshell I'm about to drop on it. I march over, fingers poised above the keyboard like a pianist ready to play a symphony...or maybe a requiem.

"Dear HR," I type, each word punctuated with purpose, "I hereby resign my position effective immediately." The keys click-clack under my touch, echoing in the empty space.

I scan the email once, twice, then hit send before I lose my nerve. It's out there now, floating through the digital ether to seal my fate.

I slam the laptop shut with more force than necessary. It's done. I'm free from his clutches, from his suffocating 'protection.'

But freedom doesn't taste as sweet as I imagined.

It's bitter, laced with the sting of what-ifs and might-have-beens.

Tears prick my eyes, but I steel my resolve. Let him realize he's screwed up royally. Because guess what? This girl isn't anyone's damsel in distress.

I swipe at the tears that betray my true feelings. Merrick—damn him—had somehow crept under my skin, into spaces reserved for whimsical daydreams and unguarded moments. But no more. I refuse to let my heart get tangled in his barbed wire again.

Abby

THE NIGHTCLUB ISN'T where I imagined I'd be again, but there's a certain power in returning to the familiar.

Pushing through the doors of the club is like stepping into another world—one of pulsating lights, thumping bass, and the tangy scent of spilled cocktails and possibility. It's like I never left, and yet everything feels different now.

I'm different now.

"Abby, you're back!" Lisa, one of the dancers, exclaims as she throws her arms around me. Her perfume, a mix of jasmine and something sinfully sweet, wraps around me like a welcome.

"Couldn't stay away," I quip, though my smile doesn't quite reach my eyes. The truth is a clawing thing inside me, desperate to break free, but I cage it with every ounce of will I have. They can't know that I'm back because my boss—no, ex-boss—couldn't respect boundaries if they were drawn in neon paint.

"Girl, we missed you! What happened? Did the corporate world chew you up and spit you out?" Jake, the bartender with a smirk that could incite sin, leans across the counter, his curiosity blatant.

I don't answers. Instead, I tie on my apron, feeling the weight of the fabric against my hips like a familiar friend—or chains. The bottles lined up behind the bar call to me, each one promising a temporary escape from reality. I grab a shaker, ice clinking musically against the metal, and I'm back in the game. Pour, mix, flirt—the motions come back to me as naturally as breathing.

Drink after drink, I pour my soul into my craft, garnishing each glass with a twist of lime and a shot of sass. The patrons eat it up, their laughter and cheers fueling me, reminding me that I am strong, capable, and damn good at my job.

But even as I bask in the nightlife's electric glow, I can't shake the shadow of Merrick. His presence is like a ghost at the edges of my consciousness, haunting me with what-ifs and memories best left forgotten.

"Hit me with your best shot," a regular winks, sliding onto a stool with the ease of familiarity.

"Careful what you wish for," I tease back, my fingers wrapping around a bottle of tequila like an old friend. "I pack a punch."

"Damn, Abby, where've you been hiding that fire?" a coworker shouts over the din, and I toss him a saucy wink.

"Wasn't hiding it, darling," I shoot back, "just had it on simmer."

But the heat cranks up a notch when I spot him—Merrick. Lurking in the shadows, his eyes are twin storms brewing on the horizon, dark and fathomless. He watches, unblinking, and the air crackles with an intensity that pulls at me, begging for the storm to break.

My heart skips, a traitorous little thing, but I stamp down the flutter. Not today, heart. We have standards now—like not falling for men who treat privacy like a suggestion.

"Another round!" a voice calls, and I'm back, the queen of my domain, drowning Merrick's gaze in a sea of vodka tonics and whiskey sours.

Merrick's stare is heavy, a tangible touch skimming across my skin. I shudder, but not from fear. No, it's something far more dangerous—anticipation, laced with defiance.

I won't cave. I can't.

Who is Merrick anyway? He's just a man.

A brooding, intense man with a gaze that could scorch the soul.

A man who I'm going to ignore, I remind myself.

The bass thumps a wild rhythm, matching the erratic beat of my heart as I maneuver through the sea of writhing bodies to deliver an order.

"Hey, sugar," drawls a voice, thick with booze and bravado. I don't need to look to know who it is; the guy's been eyeing me like I'm the last drop in an empty bottle all night.

"Keep it sweet, or keep it moving," I shoot back with a wink, placing his vodka tonic on the sticky counter. But then his hand snakes around my waist, grip tightening, pulling me a hairbreadth too close for comfort.

"Come on, baby, show me a good time," he slurs, his breath hot against my ear.

My skin crawls, every alarm bell in my head screaming red alert. I'm about to give him a piece of my mind—with interest—when suddenly, there's a shift in the atmosphere. A presence behind me, strong and silent as a storm cloud.

"Back off," rumbles a voice, low and lethal. *Merrick.*

The drunk stumbles backward as if struck, mumbling apologies before losing himself in the crowd. I'm shaking, adrenaline surging, but when I spin around, there he is—Merrick, my unexpected knight in a tailored suit.

"Thanks, but I could have handled it," I mutter, even though gratitude is a bitter pill right now.

Merrick just nods, those soulful eyes of his searching mine. There's so much there: regret, longing, a fierce protectiveness that has no right to stir anything in me. But damn it, it does.

"Abby," he starts, voice rough like gravel, but I hold up a hand.

"Save it," I say, even as my resolve wavers under the intensity of his gaze. It's like looking into the sun—blinding, burning, impossible to ignore.

"Can we talk?" His words are simple but they slice through the noise, straight to the core of me.

"Talk is cheap, Merrick." My voice is steady, but inside I'm a mess of tangled emotions.

"Please," he says, and oh, how that word wraps around my heart, tugging at strings I thought I'd severed.

I study him, really look at him. The way his jaw clenches, the slight tremor in his hands—he's a wreck, and despite everything, I care. Because beneath the layers of hurt and betrayal, there's something raw and real that pulls at me.

"Fine," I acquiesce, voice barely above the din. "But this doesn't change anything."

"Understood," he replies, but there's a glimmer of hope in his eyes that wasn't there before.

I let him lead me to a quieter corner of the club.

We stand there staring at one another. His gaze rakes over me. I note the way his chest heaves up and down.

He looks at my lips.

I look at his.

I subconsciouly lick my lips.

And then he's on me.

His lips crash into mine, and I forget why I was ever mad at him.

His hand fists in my hair, tipping my head back so he can kiss and suck on my neck.

I wrap my arms around his neck and hold on in surrender, loving the way his tongue laves at me, the way his teeth rake across my flesh.

"Mine. You're fucking mine, Abby. Do you hear me?"

I don't even try to pretend I don't love this because I do. I love the way Merrick is obsessed with me. The way he stalks me. The way he growls and warns other men away from me. The way he wants to take care of me.

I love him.

It's as if he's inside my head and mirroring my thoughts because he confesses brokenly. "I love you, Abby," as he hoists me in his arms and wraps my legs around him.

I feel his hardness pressing against me through our clothes as I confess too, "I love you too."

"Fuck," he hisses out as he begins to hump me through our clothes like a rabid animal.

I moan into his ear. "Fuck me hard and then spank me for quitting. Punish me, Merrick."

He growls a muffled curse and then he's unzipping his pants faster than the speed of light.

He doesn't even bother to touch me or prep me. He just rips my panties off, spreads my legs and say a prayer because here he comes, pounding me hard against the wall.

I moan as I feel him splitting me in two. He's so big and I'm so wet, but it feels so good, so perfect, so right.

"Fuck, Abby," he growls as he slams into me again and again, my back arching against the wall.

It's like the short time we spent apart has made us both a bit feral. Like we've both been starved of each other's touch.

"Yes, Merrick," I moan. "Fuck me harder. Harder!"

He obliges, his cock slamming into me relentlessly, his hips slapping against mine as he pounds me into oblivion.

"You're mine," he growls again.

"Yours," I agree, not even caring if the patrons in the nightclub see or hear us. All I care about is the way Merrick is driving his cock into me, hittting that special spot over and over again. The way his eyes are blazing into mine with that possessive, feral glint.

"I'm never going to let you go," he vows. "Never going to let you out of my sight again. You belong to me now. You understand? I'm going to take care of you now, Abby. No if's, and's or but's about it. You got that, baby?"

All I can do is nod and let out a keening sound as I come in an orgasmic blaze of light.

I vaguely hear Merrick praising me through my orgasm, and then he triggers another one when he reaches his own climax, his hot release jetting into me setting me off again.

I slump in his arms, my entire body jelly.

I feel him place a kiss on my forehead. "I'm taking you home," he whispers against my ear.

And for once, I don't argue with him. I'm done fighting it. He's right. I belong to him.

EPILOGUE

Six Months Later

Merrick

THE GLINT of the city lights below us is nothing compared to the electricity between Abby and me. The penthouse, with its walls adorned in modern art and furniture that screams a fortune, fades to the background as I lose myself in her kiss. My hands can't help but wander, tracing the softness of her skin, relishing in the way she shivers and sighs into my mouth.

My wife.

"God, Merrick," she breathes out, her voice a melody that stirs something primal within me.

"Abby," I murmur back, my lips never straying far from hers. It's more than her name. It's an invocation, a silent plea for more. She responds by pressing closer, her curves melding into my hard lines in a perfect puzzle of passion.

I guide her back, steps deliberate, until the backs of her knees hit the edge of the bed. With a gentle nudge, I coax her down onto the plush duvet, our embrace never breaking. We tumble together, a tangle of limbs wrapped in desire that escalates with each second we spend devouring each other.

"Your bed's as big as my entire apartment was," she quips between kisses, her humor a spark in the heat of our connection.

"And yet it still feels too small to contain what I feel for you," I counter, my voice low and laced with the truth of my heart.

Abby laughs, the sound mingling with the rustle of fabric as we move against each other. Our entwined figures carve out a space in this world that belongs only to us, a sanctum of silk sheets and unspoken promises.

My hands blaze a trail down Abby's sides, the heat from her skin seeping into my palms like sunshine. Fabric bunches and slips away under my fingers, each piece of her clothing falling to the floor with a whisper, baring her to my eyes, to my desires. Her breath catches, a sweet hitch that echoes in the vastness of the room, as my mouth wanders the expanse of her neck.

She gasps when I find that tender spot just beneath her ear, painting it with the heat of my lips. The sound of my name on her lips is a caress all its own, pushing me deeper into the realm of craving.

"Every inch of you..." I murmur against her skin, "I want to memorize how you feel, how you react." My words are hot breaths, fueling the fire that dances under her flesh.

Her chest rises and falls rapidly, her heart a drumbeat calling to my own. I watch, fascinated, as her nipples bead into tight peaks at the mere brush of my thumbs. They beg for attention, and who am I to deny such sweet pleas? Encircling them with my fingers, I tease gently, eliciting a moan that vibrates through the both of us.

"Please, more," she arches into me, an offering, a demand, her back curving like a bow pulled taut.

"Patience," I chide softly, though every fiber of my being screams to comply. My hand trails lower, a deliberate path of discovery, skirting the edge where soft thigh meets the promise of heaven. A shiver ripples through her, and I can't help but smile, knowing I'm the one to unravel Abby, this fierce, beautiful woman who matches my intensity stroke for stroke.

"Keep teasing me like that, and patience will be off

the table," she warns, her voice laced with need and a wicked sort of glee that sets my pulse racing.

"Is that a challenge?" I raise a brow, even as I continue my torturous exploration, reveling in the power I have to make her ache for me.

"Maybe," she breathes out, her eyes dark with desire and something fiercer—trust. She trusts me with her body, her pleasure, and that's more intoxicating than the finest whiskey.

"Then challenge accepted." I seal the vow with a kiss, deep and consuming.

My fingers slip lower, finding her slick with desire—a testament to the urgency of our need. I delve into her warmth, and a moan spills from her lips like sin itself. Waves of pleasure ripple through Abby's body, each one a surge I control with the dance of my digits.

"Merrick," she gasps, her voice a ragged whisper that fuels the fire within me.

"Shh, love," I murmur, focusing on the rhythm we've found together. It's a dance as old as time, yet fresh with the novelty of our passion. My heart hammers in my chest, pounding out a beat that mirrors the movement of my fingers. Her wetness coats them, the slick sound of our bodies mingling is music to my ears.

"More... please," she pleads, her hips canting towards my hand, seeking deeper, harder.

"You know I'm going to take care of you," I promise, and I mean it. Every breath, every heartbeat is dedicated to this—bringing her to the precipice where only pleasure exists.

Her back arches, a silent beg for release, and I can't deny her any longer. With a kiss to her inner thigh, I replace my fingers with my mouth, tasting her sweetness. My tongue flicks against her most sensitive spot, drawing a sharp inhale from Abby's parted lips.

"Fuck, yes..." It's a fervent whisper that stokes the fire in my veins. The sheets twist in her fists, a white-knuckle grip that tells me I'm doing everything right.

I lavish attention on her, learning the language of her body with each lap of my tongue. My name falls from her lips like a prayer, or maybe a curse—it's hard to tell when I'm lost in the taste of her.

"More, Merrick, I'm so close," Abby pants, and I can hear the edge in her voice—the brink of ecstasy.

"Let go," I command against her skin, and she shatters. Her release washes over her in waves, her body convulsing with the force of it. I hold her through it all, my mouth a constant source of pleasure until she's trembling, spent.

"Fuck," I breathe out, awestruck by the power of her climax, feeling the echo of it in my own body. The depth of my longing for her grows with each shared moment like this—raw and beautiful and utterly ours.

I slide up until I'm hovering over her. The air between us crackles with electric anticipation. I position myself, the head of my arousal nudging against her. I enter her slowly, a low groan vibrating from deep within my chest.

"God, you're so tight," I rasp out, each inch I claim in her warmth stretching the both of us to an exquisite tension.

Abby's response is a moan that seems to drag the very soul from her body. Her nails find purchase on my back, scoring down my skin in a delicious sting that sends jolts of pleasure-pain straight to my groin. "Merrick..." It's a plea, a command, everything all at once.

I set a rhythm, rocking into her with controlled thrusts, each movement deeper than the last. Our breathing syncs, labored and heavy, punctuated by the sounds of flesh meeting flesh. The world narrows down to this room, this bed, this woman whose body sings beneath mine.

"More," she gasps, and I comply, my strokes becoming more insistent, more demanding. The slick slide of our bodies together is the perfect dance.

"Fuck, Abby, you feel incredible," I grunt, my voice hoarse with desire.

"Yours," she breathes out, and that single word is my undoing. It's all the permission I need to let go, to lose myself in the tidal wave of passion that threatens to break over us.

Our movements grow frenzied, desperate, as if we can't get close enough, can't become one fast enough. Her cries crescendo with each thrust, urging me on, and I anchor myself in the heat of her gaze, the unspoken promises reflected there.

"Come with me," I urge between gritted teeth, feeling the pressure build at the base of my spine.

She meets my eyes, nodding, her body clenching around me in sweet surrender. As I watch the ecstasy wash over her face, her inner walls fluttering around me, I'm catapulted over the edge into blinding pleasure. We shudder together, a perfect storm of sensation that obliterates thought, coherent words, everything except the here and now.

As the ripples of our climax subside, leaving us gasping and clinging to each other, I collapse beside her, pulling Abby close. Her heartbeat drums against my chest, a testament to the intensity of what we've shared.

"Damn," she whispers, a satisfied smile tugging at her lips.

"Understatement of the century," I manage to say, still reeling. And for a long moment, we just lie there, basking in the afterglow.

I brush a lock of hair from Abby's forehead, my

chest swelling with something so fierce it could be nothing other than love. Her eyelids flutter open, revealing pools of liquid chocolate, deep and warm. In them, I see my future—*our* future.

"Abby," my voice comes out hoarse, raw from passion, "I want everything with you. A lifetime of mornings like this, nights that never end..." My throat tightens as I say the words that have been burning inside me, "I want to fill our lives with mini versions of us, to build a family together."

Her eyes widen, but they don't waver. They anchor me, hold me steady in their gaze. "Merrick, you're my heart," she says, her voice soft as silk, strong as steel. "I've never been more certain of anything."

We lie there, wrapped in each other, skin on skin, hearts melded together. The silence is comfortable, filled with the symphony of our synchronized breathing. I trace patterns on her back, marveling at how natural it feels to consider a future with Abby. Not just any future, but one with laughter ringing through the halls, little feet pattering about, and her, always her, by my side.

"Tell me," I murmur, "what do you dream about for us?"

She props herself up on an elbow, her hair cascading around her shoulders like a dark waterfall. "I dream of a home filled with love, where every corner holds a memory we've made." Abby bites her lip, a playful glint in her eye. "And I dream of making those memories everywhere...the kitchen, the living room, even the garden."

"Naughty and nice," I chuckle, pulling her close again. "I love that about you."

"Good," she says, her fingers tracing the lines of my chest, "because I plan on keeping you on your toes, Mr. Mason. Every step of the way."

"Is that a promise, Mrs. Mason?" I tease, already envisioning a life of chasing this incredible woman through all our tomorrows.

"Absolutely," Abby whispers against my lips before sealing her promise with a kiss.

———

I lean back in my leather chair and watch Abby as she pores over the spreadsheets scattered across the desk, her brow furrowing with concentration. I can't help the smirk tugging at the corner of my mouth. Who would've thought that Abby, free-spirited and wild, would have such a knack for numbers?

"Got it!" she exclaims, looking up at me with triumphant eyes. "If we streamline the distribution process like this," she taps the paper with her pen, "we'll increase efficiency by at least fifteen percent."

"Damn, you're good," I say, genuinely impressed. Our business meetings have been more productive since Abby joined the fray. She's not just decoration in my office. She's become the brain behind some of our best moves.

"Wait till you see what else I'm good at," she teases with a playful wink.

And just like that, the air between us crackles with electricity. The numbers on the papers might as well be ancient hieroglyphs because there's no way I can focus on them now—not with the way Abby's tongue darts out to wet her lips, a subtle promise of what's to come.

"Is that so?" My voice drops an octave as I stand and make my way around the desk. Her eyes follow my every move, darkening with desire.

"Absolutely," she whispers, and in two long strides, I'm right in front of her, pulling her up by the hands so her body crashes into mine.

"Show me," I growl against her lips before our mouths collide in a fevered kiss. She tastes like the caramel latte she nursed earlier, sweet and addictive. It doesn't take long before our kisses turn into something more primal, more urgent.

Clothes are shed without ceremony, and soon, Abby's back is against the cold, hard surface of the desk. It's a stark contrast to the heat we generate together. As I enter her, the sleek lines of professionalism in our office blur into a mess of passion. I move with a purpose, each thrust punctuating the silent promises of forever we make in the quiet afterglow of our bedroom every night.

"Merrick," Abby moans, her legs wrapped tightly around me. She meets me stroke for stroke, a perfect symphony of lust and love.

"Abby..." I groan her name like a mantra, feeling the familiar tightening coil of pleasure. We chase our climax together, breathless and unabashed in our need for one another.

As we crest the wave, our climax shatters through us, a shared explosion of ecstasy that seems to shake the very foundations of the office building. I collapse onto her, our sweat-mingled bodies heaving, trying to catch lost breaths.

"Wow," she breathes out, her fingers lazily drawing circles on my back.

"Wow, indeed," I agree, pressing a soft kiss to her forehead. I pull off her, but keep her close, needing the contact.

"Partner in life and in business," she murmurs, her head resting against my chest.

"Best damn partnership I've ever had," I reply, my hand finding hers and giving it a squeeze.

"Ready to go again, Mr. Mason?" Abby asks, the glint in her eyes promising round two.

"Always, Mrs. Mason," I quip back, capturing her lips in another passionate kiss—a promise sealed, our future laid bare in the heart of our shared empire.

Always.

Want a free book from Emma Bray? Go to www. authoremmabray.com.